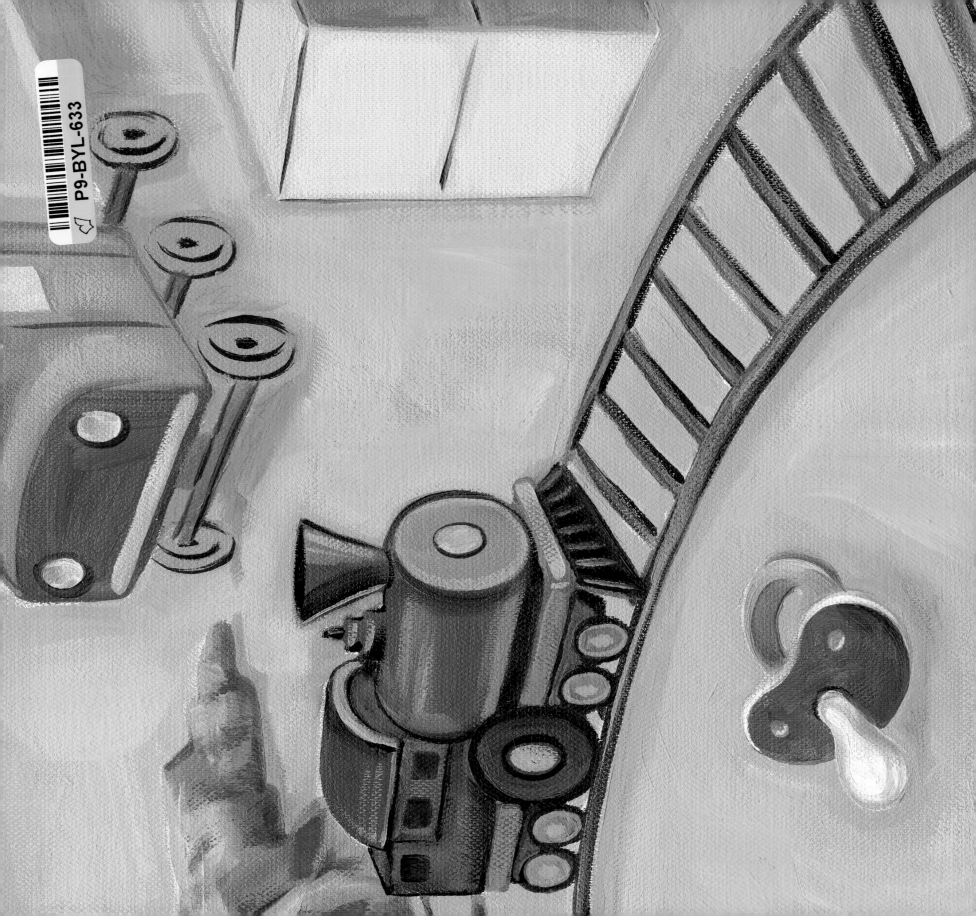

llama llama time to share

Anna Dewdney

VIKING

An Imprint of Penguin Group (USA) Inc.

Llama Llama playing trains, driving trucks, and flying planes.

Someone's at the door . . . . who is it?
Brand new neighbors come to visit.

Look!

Llama, this is Nelly Gnu.

She has a dolly, too.

Mrs. Gnu, would you like tea?

Come and have a cup with me.

You two kids can play in there. . . .

And Llama,
don't forget to **share.**

Trains and trucks and puzzles, too.
What's the Gnu girl want to do?
Play with kitchen? Build with blocks?
Llama opens up his box.

Nelly starts to build a town.
Llama Llama starts to frown. . . . .

Nelly Gnu makes walls and stairs.
Llama watches from a chair.

Nelly stacks the blocks up high.
Fuzzy Llama wants to try.

It's a castle! Make it tall.
Fuzzy Llama jumps the wall!

Build a tower. Make a moat.
Nelly's dolly rows a boat.

What can Llama Llama add?
Maybe sharing's **not** so bad.

Little baby Gnu makes noise.
Mrs. Gnu gets jingly toys.
Baby screams and kicks his feet.
Mama thinks it's time to eat.

Moms are talking,
baby's chewing. . . .

Where's that Gnu girl?
What's **she** doing?

Oh, **disaster!** Dolly drama!

Nelly Gnu has
Fuzzy Llama!

He's not hers! This isn't fair!

Llama DOESN'T

LIKE to share!

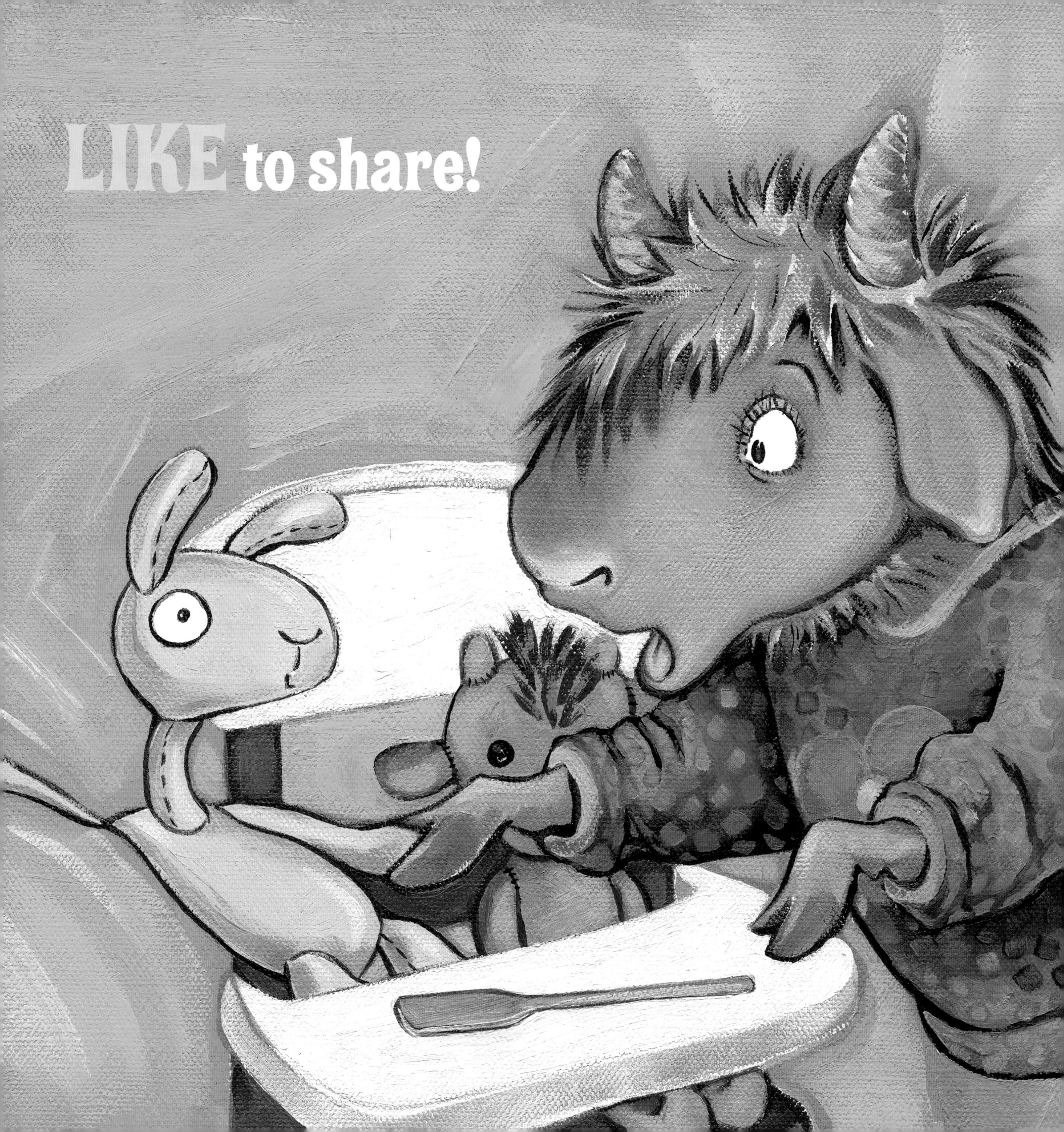

Fuzzy Llama ripped in two . . . all because of Nelly Gnu!

It's a llama-mergency!

Mama! Fix his arm for me!

A bit of thread and good as new . . . . . but this is what we're going to do:

I'll put Fuzzy on the stairs
until you're **sure** that you can share.

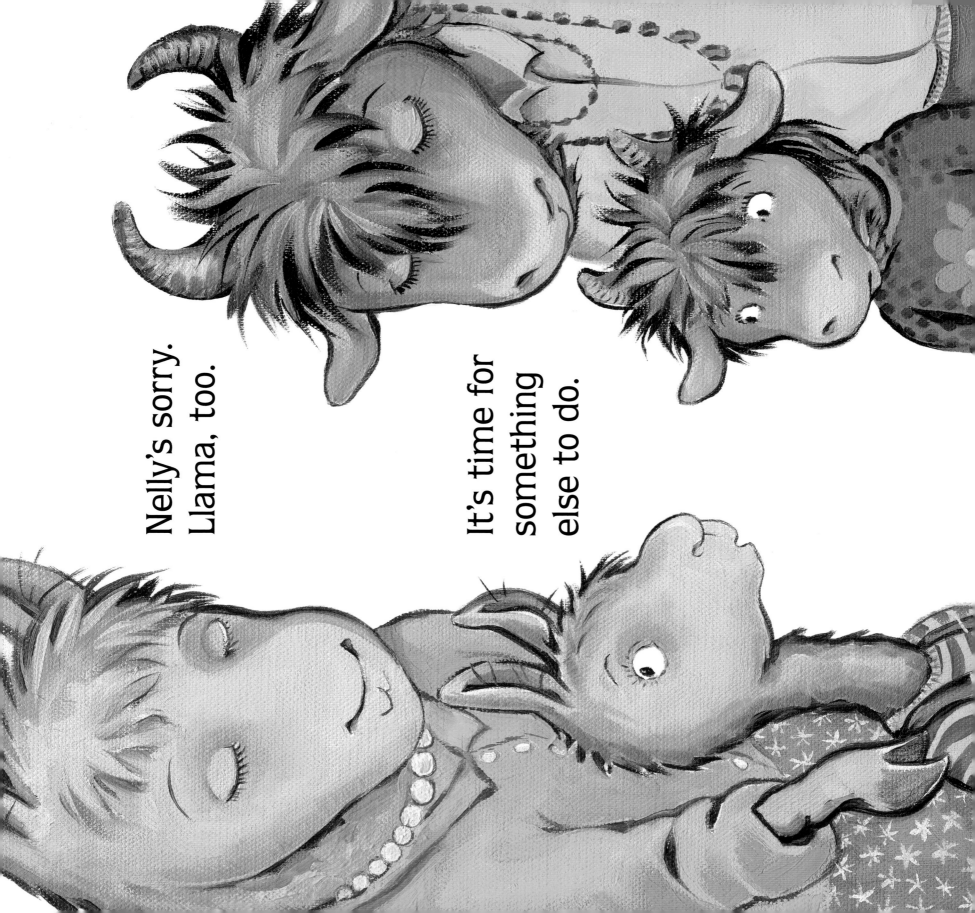

Nelly's sorry. Llama, too.

It's time for something else to do.

Like to dress up?

Not a lot.

Maybe tractors?

Maybe not.

Let's play kitchen!
Make a cake!

Nelly mixes. Llama bakes.

Look—our fancy cake is done!

Hmmm . . .
what would make this game **more** fun?

Fuzzy Llama, on the stairs!

Llama thinks it's **time to share.**

Playtime's over. It's the end . . . .

but Llama has a brand new friend.

Nelly will be back, and then . . . .

Llama wants to **share again!**

To my sister Alice, with love

VIKING
Published by the Penguin Group
Penguin Young Readers Group, 345 Hudson Street, New York, New York 10014, U.S.A.
Penguin Group (Canada), 90 Eglinton Avenue East, Suite 700, Toronto, Ontario, Canada M4P 2Y3
(a division of Pearson Penguin Canada Inc.)
Penguin Books Ltd, 80 Strand, London WC2R 0RL, England
Penguin Ireland, 25 St Stephen's Green, Dublin 2, Ireland (a division of Penguin Books Ltd)
Penguin Group (Australia), 250 Camberwell Road, Camberwell, Victoria 3124, Australia
(a division of Pearson Australia Group Pty Ltd)
Penguin Books India Pvt Ltd, 11 Community Centre, Panchsheel Park, New Delhi – 110 017, India
Penguin Group (NZ), 67 Apollo Drive, Rosedale, Auckland 0632, New Zealand (a division of Pearson New Zealand Ltd.)
Penguin Books (South Africa) (Pty) Ltd, 24 Sturdee Avenue, Rosebank, Johannesburg 2196, South Africa

Penguin Books Ltd, Registered Offices: 80 Strand, London WC2R 0RL, England

First published in the United States of America by Viking, a division of Penguin Young Readers Group, 2012

24

Copyright © 2012 by the Anna E. Dewdney Literary Trust
All rights reserved

LIBRARY OF CONGRESS CATALOGING-IN-PUBLICATION DATA
Dewdney, Anna.
Llama Llama time to share / Anna Dewdney.
p. cm.
Summary: "Llama Llama doesn't want to share his toys with his new neighbors. But when fighting leads to broken toys and tears,
Llama learns that it's better to share"—Provided by publisher.
ISBN 978-0-670-01233-6 (hardback)
[1. Stories in rhyme. 2. Sharing—Fiction. 3. Llamas—Fiction.] I. Title.
PZ8.3.D498Lgd 2012   [E]—dc23   2012001431

Manufactured in China   Set in ITC Quorum

The art for this book was created with oil paint, colored pencil,
and oil pastel on primed canvas.